Inga and Olaf: Modern Parables

by

James D. Rapp

Table of Contents

Foreword

It is a good thing that some "brain children" never advance beyond the stage of "a twinkle in their father's eye." They are thus saved from an ignoble existence after birth – collecting dust on the shelves of those who preserve them out of a sense of obligation to their parent. Or more likely they are saved from a necessary but undignified demise in a shredder or a garbage truck, sometimes at the hand of their own parent.

I have not been reluctant, over the years, to bring my "children" into the world, and many have suffered one of the fates just mentioned. But occasionally one parents a "child" which he or she believes to hold some promise; one that reflects, in most ways, the values of its parent. Such was the case when I wrote the first of the Inga and Olaf parables, "The Coloring Book" (originally titled "Inga and Olaf: A Modern Parable").

Primogeniture – the right of the firstborn to inherit the lion's share of the family's goods and glory – is a hallowed tradition of mankind, but one that has been violated time and again when a parent sees more promise in a younger child than is evident in the firstborn. So, after the birth of its younger siblings, "Inga and Olaf: A Modern Parable" was required to donated its original name to serve as the title of the collective work. Adding to the indignity of accepting a new name, "The Coloring Book," it also was forced to relinquished its "birthright" – its place in line – to "The Diary".

Not unlike the parents of real children, I conceived the first of these stories "just for fun." Those that came later were more deliberately planned to fit into the family and fill out its purpose.

And what is that purpose?

I would be less than honest if I said the purpose was always evident to me. Most of the stories grew out of situations I was concerned with at the time and it seemed to help me work through those problems – usually they were problems – if I could allow Inga and Olaf to struggle with them.

And why Inga and Olaf?

My life has been spent in two geographic areas of the United States, central Illinois and Minnesota-Wisconsin. From my mother, primarily, I learned to speak my native tongue, generic American. From friends and relatives in Illinois I learned to imitate a Southern accent. And from certain residents of Minnesota-Wisconsin I learned the sounds and cadences of Scandinavian accent. Olaf and Inga, with their peculiar ethnic phrasings, seemed the perfect voices to express the ideas in these parables.

Readers not familiar with Norwegian immigrant speech patterns may either miss that aspect of the stories or simply think the phrasing peculiar or incorrect. Those very familiar with Norwegian-American accent may complain that they are too muted in these stories. Perhaps a little history of the development of the stories is in order.

The original parables were written as dramatic skits to be performed, heavily accented, by two actors. At the time I wrote them I was co-directing dramas with Cheryl Brandt who, by the way, deserves considerable credit for the development of the characters as well as input into the central themes of several of the pieces. My first attempt to convert the skits to short story format involved no more than adding the short narrative sections and the "he said," "she said" dialogue indicators. The heavy accents were retained and indicated in the text by phonetic spellings.

It became evident that such accenting, while delightful and informative in a performance, where one had only to listen, was a great hindrance to flow and understanding when one was required to decipher it from the page. So the decision was made to eliminate the accents and try instead to capture some of the flavor of Norwegian-American phrasing and colloquialism.

But it is the authenticity of the characters and their life situations that I hope to have conveyed in these stories. The authenticity of the human situation crosses all barriers of language and dialect. Even of culture. Inga speaks to all of us. And Olaf, especially, speaks *for* all of us. *Inga and Olaf: Modern Parables* reminds us of where we have been and what we need to return to.

Jim Rapp – February, 4, 2011

Prologue

Olaf was not unintelligent, but those who knew him would have been hard-pressed to prove it. Age had not healed the self-inflicted wounds of Olaf's early years.

As a child he found school boring, and thus difficult. Rather than struggle to learn the skills he would need for success in life, or take the help offered by his teachers and his sister, Inga, he chose instead to follow the path many boys in his time did. The result was an early end to his schooling, and escape from home and family.

Menial jobs around town bought Olaf an assortment of meager living conditions over the years. But most of his pay went to support evenings, spent drinking with his buddies, living "the good life," and barely keeping ahead of the law.

Eventually age brought some sobriety to Olaf's life. He found a permanent job with a local garbage collection company, working up the ranks to claim his own route which he proudly "managed" for the last 20 years before his retirement.

Those who had known him since his youth saw Olaf slowly change from a rowdy bar hopper to a lonely middle-aged man. The companions of his youth were gone. A few of his drinking buddies had not survived into middle age as he had. Those who did had seen the error of their ways and had become productive citizens and workers in the community, moving in circles Olaf could not navigate. Olaf was a relic of his early years.

But age, which had brought a measure of sobriety, had not made Olaf any wiser or better informed. Though he was well liked and trusted by his bosses and the customers on his route, his interactions with them were on a superficial plane. He struggled to read and write, and his knowledge of anything that required reading was sorely lacking. As a result he regularly connected the effects in his life with the wrong causes. Olaf was fair game for a ruse or a scam. So, more and more, he kept to himself, and to his six pack, avoiding situations in which he could be taken advantage of. Fishing and watching televised sporting events defined the edges of Olaf's existence.

The family that Olaf left in his youth included one sister, Inga. Inga was creative, as their father had been. The house that Olaf left in his youth, the Ingabretson House, was a landmark in town. Inga lived there, pursuing interests their father had pursued, writing and painting; keeping alive knowledge of his work. Inga was known, as her father had been, as one who could be counted on, in a time of trouble, to speak an honest word, or do a helpful deed. But it was not uncommon for her to overhear someone remark, to her great sorrow, that she and her brother Olaf were so different as to make one wonder if they came from the same father.

Though Olaf had assiduously sought to avoid contact with his sister, she had often sought him out over the years, urging him to return and live with her in the old family home. The Olaf she had known in his childhood held a promise that the years had squandered, and she longed to recover the goodness she knew was latent in him. But the years of separation, and the sense of betrayal that Olaf carried in his mind, kept him at a guilty distance from the love that Inga longed to shower on him.

The stories that follow tell, mostly in the siblings' own words, the journey Olaf made back to Inga, the Ingabretson House, and ultimately to his father.

The Diary

"Olaf! Are you feeling alright?" Inga asked.

"Ya, Inga. I am okay," Olaf replied.

Olaf was visiting at his sister Inga's house again. Thirty years ago the Ingabretson House had been his home too. He had missed the old house since he left, but more, he had missed his sister Inga. Not that they never saw each other, and not that Inga never tried to persuade him to return. But pride had kept him from returning – pride, and a fear that his return would spell the end to other friendships he valued. And more than all, Olaf could not forget the reason that he left.

But lately he had begun stopping by. Over the weeks his visits became more prolonged; he began to feel more "at home." But he nonetheless stoutly resisted Inga's invitations to really make it his home again.

Today though, Olaf had come for dinner and was lingering as evening approached. Inga had cleared away the dishes and settled in the parlor to read a book. Olaf, never one to read much, nonetheless found himself thumbing through their father's old diary that Inga had left lying strategically on a table.

Several minutes had passed before Inga became aware that Olaf was sniffling as he labored to read the words of the diary.

Laying her book aside Inga went to sit by Olaf.

"What is that you are reading, Olaf? You seem very interested in it."

"I'm reading Father's diary that was laying here … the part when we were just youngsters."

"Oh, Olaf, those were such wonderful days when we were just kids together. I remember what a happy boy you were, and how much I loved you and admired you."

"Ya Inga, you were a wonderful sister too." Olaf hesitated, then continued, "I don't remember you ever being bad … I don't think you ever were bad, Inga."

"Oh, Olaf, that is so good of you to say. I think I just mainly wanted to please Father, and that helped me to be good."

Inga's words created an awkward pause. Inga knew the thoughts in Olaf's mind. She wanted to talk to him about them but she would wait until Olaf was ready.

"Olaf," she said, "I'm so glad you came by today. I was wondering when you would come again. I wish you would come here to live with me in Father's house."

Olaf said nothing.

Inga sensed his discomfort. She moved to sit by him.

"Olaf, read me some of the parts of Father's diary that you like the best. I would love to hear them."

Olaf demurred, closing the book defensively. "No, Inga! I … I couldn't! I … I don't read good like you do."

"Sure you can, Olaf," she assured him. "I love to read Father's diary. There are parts that make me laugh and parts that make me cry, but I love them all because Father put them there for us. He wanted us to know all the things that are in his diary."

Olaf clung to the diary, holding its cover shut.

"Inga, I think there are far more things there to make me cry than there are to make me laugh."

"Like what, Olaf?" Inga prodded.

"Well," Olaf responded, "when I read all the things that Father had planned for my life, the hopes he had for me …" He paused to let the lump in his throat subside. "And then I think of the things I've done with it … with my life. That makes me sad."

"Yes, Olaf …"

Olaf continued, "And when I read about the things I did to you, Inga … well, it makes it hard for me to even look you in the eyes."

Inga reached out and took Olaf's hand.

"Oh, Olaf. I want you to always be able to look me in the eyes. I have forgiven you for everything bad you ever did to me."

"Ya, that's all good enough," Olaf sniffled, wiping his nose on his sleeve, "but I don't think I can ever forgive myself for the things I have done to you …"

There was a long pause. Inga knew that the moment she was waiting for had come, but she waited for Olaf to go on.

"Inga," Olaf continued, "do you remember those things I did?"

"Yes, Olaf. I remember. They made Father and me very sad."

"I'm afraid I was very bad to both of you …" Olaf confessed.

Inga increased the pressure on Olaf's hand as she spoke.

"Olaf, we were not sad – Father and I – because you were not nice to us … we were sad because of what you were doing to yourself. You were … you were getting farther and farther away from us."

"What do you mean, Inga?"

When Inga said nothing, Olaf continued.

"I don't think I ever knew how much I hurt you and Father until I read about it in this here diary …"

Inga waited. Olaf struggled to go on.

"I mean … I could see how badly you were injured, Inga … and I knew it was my fault … and I hated those who had injured you … and … and I knew that I was one of them …"

Inga gave another squeeze to Olaf's hand to remind him that she was holding it.

"Did you know that I loved you, Olaf? Did you know that Father loved you?"

"How could you love me, Inga?" Olaf asked incredulously. "How could Father love me? All those years that I was running with the Larson boys, and the Swenson boys, you and Father were trying to tell me how bad they were for me."

"They were bad for you, Olaf … and you were bad for them, too."

"But I never thought they would do to you what they did, Inga." Olaf protested. "I would never have been their friend if I had thought that."

"Is that true, Olaf?"

Olaf could not look at Inga. He wanted – and he did not want – to remove his hand from hers.

"No Inga, that isn't true. I resented the things you were telling us as much as they did. And when you came that time to persuade me to leave them and come home with you, I was just as angry with you as they were …"

"I know Olaf … I could see it in your eyes. I could feel it in your spirit."

"But Inga, when they began to …when I saw that they were going to …"

For a long time Olaf could not speak.

"Inga," he finally continued, "I had never seen anyone who hated so much that they would kill an innocent person …"

There was another long pause. Inga waited.

"When Father came and found you at the bottom of that cliff," Olaf continued, "when he took you in his arms to carry you home … I knew that we had killed you … that *I* had killed you."

Inga waited a long time before speaking Olaf's name.

"Olaf!"

"Ya, Inga?"

"When did you hear that Father had nursed me back to health?"

"I heard it right away, Inga." Olaf said. "At first I didn't believe it … the Larsons and the

Swensons all said it was some trick …that Father had … well, in some way he had tricked us."

"No, Olaf," Inga said, "it was no trick. It was Father's great love for me – and his great love for you too, Olaf – that brought me back."

Inga waited while Olaf thought about her words.

"Olaf," she continued, "Father's great love is calling you to come back now … It is Father's will … It is written right there in his diary … It is His will that you live here … with me … in Father's house."

"How could I do that, Inga," Olaf protested, "after all the bad things I have done to you and Father … after all the things I've said bad about you?"

"Olaf, do you love me?"

"Ya, Inga, I have always loved you …"

"Do you love Father, Olaf?"

Olaf hesitated.

"I think I do, Inga … I never knew Father as well as I knew you, though."

"You need to come and live with me in Father's house." Inga urged. "I can teach you about Father and you will come to love him just as I do, Olaf."

"Would there be room for me here, Inga?" Olaf asked hopefully. "I don't want to be in the way all the time, you know."

"Oh Olaf," Inga laughed, "that is just what Father wanted; that is just what I want. We want you to be in the way all the time. There is plenty of room here for you … there is a place made just for you."

"Oh Inga! Is that true? Would you show it to me … now?"

"Sure Olaf!" Inga pulled Olaf up from his chair. "You just come with me and I'll show you. It isn't complete yet Olaf. Father wanted you to have a part in finishing it …"

Olaf hesitated, holding back.

"Inga, I'm so sorry for all the things I said … all the things I did that hurt you and Father … will you forgive me for what I have done?"

"Oh sure, Olaf," Inga said. "We forgave you on that day long ago … we have just been waiting for you to come home."

The Coloring Book

It was Sunday afternoon and Olaf was not watching a Packer game, but Inga hadn't notice it right away.

In the year since Olaf returned to live with his sister at the old Ingabretson House, their lives had settled into familiar routines, especially on Sunday afternoons – Inga working at her easel, with her back to the TV, Olaf watching some sporting event, preferably the Green Bay Packers.

But this day was different. Inga slowly became aware that her mind was not competing with the din of shouting fans or Olaf's grunts of approval or dismay; Olaf was working quietly and diligently at the dining room table.

Speaking over her shoulder Inga asked, "Olaf, why aren't you watching the Packer's game today?"

"Inga, you don't have to rub it in," Olaf replied brusquely.

"I don't know what you mean, Olaf," Inga said, sincerely puzzled. "I was just asking a simple question. You don't have to get terse with me."

"I think you know, Inga, that the Packers are out of the play-offs," Olaf countered, still not convinced that Inga wasn't teasing him.

"Oh yes! Now that you mention it, I do remember that they lost," said Inga, returning to her work. "That's too bad, Olaf. But there must be another game on today that you could be watching."

"Ya! I know," Olaf replied, softening his tone, convinced now that Inga was sincere. "But I have something more important that I'm working on today."

Inga laid aside her brush and, wiping her hands on her apron, moved to the table where Olaf was laboring. "Oh, what is that, Olaf?" she said, trying to peer over his shoulder." "I'd love to see it."

"Well, it isn't very good, Inga." Olaf shielded his work and looked back at Inga's easel. "I'm not as good as you."

"Let me see, Olaf," Inga gently coaxed. "Tell me what it is you are doing."

"No Inga, you will think it is bad …"

"Olaf, have I ever made fun of anything you did?"

"No," Olaf admitted, still holding his hand over his work. "But you have never seen this."

"Well, Olaf, then just tell me what it is you are doing."

Olaf picked up a newspaper and pointed to an advertisement.

"You see this ad, Inga?" he said, "It says here they are having a Green Bay Packer coloring book contest and the child … the person that colors the best picture will have it displayed in the Oakwood Mall and he will win a genuine Green Bay Packer game ball signed by Bret Farve. I went right to the Wal-Mart and bought a Green Bay coloring book."

Olaf opened the coloring book for Inga to see.

"There Inga, what do you think of that?"

There was an embarrassed silence while Inga examined Olaf's coloring.

"Well **…**" she finally said.

"You don't like it, do you Inga?," Olaf asked. "You think it's bad …"

"Oh, Olaf … I think …"

Inga picked up the book and looked more closely. She wanted to affirm Olaf but be truthful too.

"Let me think about this …"

Olaf took the book back from Inga. His shoulders sagged.

"No, Inga. I know it is not good. I never could stay within the lines … and look there … see that color? It isn't anything like what I wanted."

Olaf turned again to look at Inga's easel.

"Inga, why can you paint such wonderful pictures and I can't?"

"Olaf, I learned everything I know from Father."

Inga put her hands gently on Olaf's shoulders.

"I'm still learning from him, reading his book and looking at the pictures he painted … I would be no artist at all if I didn't follow his example."

"Ya, I know Inga," Olaf replied. "I should have spent more time learning from him too. But I had other things I wanted to do … I thought maybe I could be a famous quarterback …"

Olaf paused, looking at Inga with resignation.

"I guess that was a pipe dream, huh Inga?"

Inga said nothing. She leaned forward and laid her cheek against his head.

"Ya, that was a pipe dream, Inga. *But now I want to win that coloring book contest!*" Olaf insisted.

Suddenly Olaf paused, as though a light had turned on.

"Inga, would you do something for me?"

"Oh Olaf! You know I would if it is something I can do," Inga said.

"Inga …" Olaf hesitated, "maybe if you … Inga, would you color a page in the book for me?"

"Sure Olaf," Inga said, "first let me get a chair …"

Inga had taken only a few steps when she stopped, turning slowly to Olaf in disbelief.

"Olaf, you don't mean … you wouldn't want me to color a picture for you to submit to the contest?" she said.

"Well, Inga, you don't know how much I want to win this contest!" Olaf protested. "It isn't just the football … I want to have people know me as a good artist."

Inga returned to the table. She spoke softly but firmly.

"But Olaf, it wouldn't be your picture. If I did it we'd have to put my name on it."

"Why not just put Ingabretson on it, we are both Ingabretsons." Olaf argued. "Then they will think it is my picture because you always paint your pictures."

Inga spoke slowly and deliberately.

"Olaf … if we did that … and if you won the contest … and the picture was hung in the Oakwood Mall … would you feel like a real artist?"

Olaf's shoulders slumped again. There was another long silence.

"No Inga … you are right! I wouldn't."

Olaf opened the coloring book and found the page he had colored. He tore out the picture, crumpled it, and sat staring at it in his clenched fist.

"It is no use, Inga … if there ever was a time when I could have been an artist it is past now. When I was young, I went outside the lines because I was in too big a hurry to get the picture done. But now that I am old and want to stay within the lines, my hands are too shaky to do it."

Inga sat down opposite Olaf. She reached across the table and put her hand over his clenched fist.

"Oh, Olaf! It is never too late to color a picture … one that you will be proud of … one that would make our Father proud. Olaf, the things I paint are the things I learned from Father. You can do that too."

Olaf looked at her with helpless disbelief.

"I can help you, Olaf," Inga assured him, giving his hand a squeeze.

It was quiet for a long time as Olaf contemplated Inga's gentle hand on his clenched fist.

"How, Inga?" he finally asked.

"Well, Olaf," Inga began enthusiastically, "I could suggest what colors might work well … and how to shade them … and I could even suggest what you might want to put in the picture … and when your hand is trembling, Olaf, and you have trouble staying in the lines, I could hold your hand and keep it steady."

"Oh Inga … would you do that for me?"

"Sure Olaf," Inga said, "let me move my chair to the other side …"

As Inga settled in her chair the tears in her eyes expressed her joy.

"You can't know, Olaf, how long I've wanted to help you with this …"

"Thank you Inga," Olaf said.

Olaf fumbled in the coloring book, looking for the picture he wanted to color.

"I think I want to color a picture," he said, "where the Packers are creaming the Vikings."

Inga laughed at Olaf as she handed him the box of crayons. She knew that Father was laughing too.

The Picture Book

"Well, Olaf!" Inga said, "What are you reading tonight? Something about the Packers I suppose."

Evenings at the Ingabretson House were unfailingly the same, Inga quietly painting or reading after her evening chores, Olaf, home from his day on the garbage route, watching some sporting event on T.V. or, failing that, exploring the old house to regain some part of their past he had relinquished in the years he lived in a self-imposed exile.

This evening Olaf found nothing of interest on T.V. so he was laboring to read a book, written by their Father, that Inga had been encouraging him to look at. Inga sensed that Olaf was struggling with something. She left her easel and sat in a chair next to him.

"No, Inga," Olaf replied, "I'm reading something you have told me for a long time that I should read."

"Oh!" Inga said, "and what would that be, Olaf."

"Well you know, Inga, you have been telling me that I should read Father's book and then I could become a good painter like you."

"That is true, Olaf," Inga responded, "I do want you to read Father's book. It will be good for you to know what is in his book, whether you become a painter or not. What do you think of it, Olaf, now that you are reading it?"

"Well, to be perfectly honest with you, Inga," Olaf said, "I'm not finding it very easy to read."

"Oh, I'm sorry Olaf. Can I help you in any way?" Inga offered.

"Well, the biggest surprise I had was that there weren't any pictures in it." Olaf's tone showed a slight sense of pique. "I thought you said that Father was a great artist, Inga. You said that the pictures you paint, you learned from Father."

"That's true, Olaf," Inga replied. "I do paint pictures that I find in Father's book. And some that I paint are just hinted at in his book. And some are not in his book at all, but I learned them all from him, just the same."

"Now you have really got me confused, Inga," Olaf said.

"Oh Olaf," Inga continued, laying a hand on his shoulder. "Father didn't put everything in his book that he wants us to know. He gave us other ways to know the things he wants us to know."

Inga's touch made Olaf aware that he was being unfairly harsh with his sister. He softened his tone.

"Well, I know, Inga, that he must have wanted me to have a wonderful sister like you."

"Thank you, Olaf," Inga said, giving his shoulder a pat. "There are lots of other people who know Father and have read his book. They can all help you understand Father's book, Olaf, if you ask them."

"Well, that's all well and good, Inga," Olaf said. "But I still don't see any pictures in this book of his. Either you took them out," he said wryly, "or they are printed with invisible ink."

"I think they are printed with invisible ink, Olaf," Inga laughed, "Invisible to you, but not to me."

"Inga, sometimes I think you enjoy teasing me," Olaf protested. "I think you make fun of me sometimes."

"Olaf. You know that I have always loved you, even when I do tease you," Inga responded. "But you must have forgotten all the times you made fun of me, and laughed at my pictures, and tried to tear them up."

"No, Inga. I haven't forgot."

Olaf was chastened by what he remembered.

"I wasn't very nice to you then. But I didn't always like the pictures you were painting. Some of them made me feel … well …"

"I understand, Olaf," Inga said, "and I forgive you. But if you could see the pictures in Father's book you would understand why I had to paint them."

Olaf remained quiet for a while, thinking of his early treatment of his sister.

"Inga, I have to tell you that the reason I … well …." Olaf fumbled for words. "I have to say I hated your pictures! You always painted pictures of Father being here with us, and I don't hardly ever remember when he was here with us."

As Olaf thought about those early years the old frustrations were expressed in his voice.

"All I remember is this book that you were always reading, and the things that you said you saw in it, and the pictures that you were always painting."

"Olaf, I knew how you felt," Inga said softly. "But I wanted you to see Father like I see him. I've always wanted you to see him in me, and in the pictures I painted. I want you to see the pictures in his book."

Olaf's shoulders sagged under her hand.

"Ya, Inga, I know," he said. "But I think it is no use. I don't see any pictures there … and I don't think I ever will. It is all … well … it is … it is just nothing!"

"Olaf, do you really want to see the pictures in the book?"

Olaf looked up imploringly. "Ya Inga, I really do …"

"Well then, if you really want to see them I could sit here with you and tell you what I see, and then I think that you will begin to see them."

"Would you do that, Inga?" Olaf asked. "I would like that."

"Sure, Olaf!" Inga said.

She moved her chair nearer to Olaf.

"I'll just get closer here and we can both see the book at the same time."

Olaf shifted the book so Inga could turn the pages.

"Here," Inga began, "here is a picture of Father at Christmas time, a long time ago. And see, he is bringing you a gift. Can you see it Olaf?"

Olaf leaned down to view the page. "Ya, Inga. I think I do see something there." Olaf said. "But I don't see any gift that Father is bringing."

"Look closely, Olaf," Inga urged. "What is it that Father has in his arms?"

"Well, it looks like a baby, Inga."

He stared at the picture for several seconds, then looked at Inga.

"Is that you?" Olaf asked. "You were born on Christmas Day, Inga … is that baby you?"

Inga laid her hand on Olaf's. "Yes, Olaf, that is me. And Father is holding me in his arms. He is giving me to you, the most precious gift he had to give you that day."

Olaf looked again at the picture, then at Inga.

"I haven't always appreciated Father's gift as much as I should have, Inga."

Olaf clumsily took Inga's hand before continuing.

"That must have made him sad. That must make you sad, Inga. Can you forgive me?"

Inga clasped his hand in both of hers.

"Oh Olaf, I have forgiven you a long, long time ago. And I forgive you now too, since you ask me."

Inga pulled the book into her lap, starting to page through it.

"Olaf, would you like to see some more pictures in Father's book?" she asked.

"Sure, Inga," Olaf nudged his chair a bit closer to hers. "You show me what you see there."

"Well, let's see what we can find," Inga said, continuing to turn the pages.

Olaf suddenly stopped her and turned back a couple of pages.

"Oh, Inga," he said, "look at that picture of Father. That is just how I remember seeing him a long time ago, when I was just a little boy."

"Yes, Olaf," Inga replied, "See how he is standing by the gate, looking down the road. That is so like how Father always was, isn't it, Olaf?"

"I wonder what he is looking for, Inga. Can you see?" Olaf asked.

Inga pointed to a place on the page.

"There is someone coming up the road, Olaf. Can you see who it is?"

Olaf squinted at the page, then looked quizzically at Inga. "That looks like it is me who is coming," he said. "Inga … is that me?"

"Yes," Inga replied "that is you, Olaf … and Father is waiting for you."

Heart's Ease

"Inga!" Olaf called out.

Inga appeared in the kitchen doorway, wiping her hands on her apron.

"Did you call me, Olaf?" she asked.

"Ya, Inga, I was wondering if you knew the zip code in Miami, Florida? They want the zip code on this here form I'm filling out."

Olaf's wayward youth had left him unprepared to handle any task involving words, especially if they exceeded a fifth-grade reading level. But he had a strong incentive this day as he struggled mightily to fill out the forms before him. He was fumbling through a thick almanac in hope of finding some information he needed.

Inga walked to the table where Olaf was working.

"Well, Olaf, the zip code for a large city like that will depend on where in Miami the place is," Inga explained. "Do you know the street number?"

"Let me see," Olaf puzzled. "It must be Box Street. 22301 Box Street."

"Let me look, Olaf," Inga said. She picked up the form from him and examined it. "No, that is not a street," Inga explained, "that is a post office box number. And there is the zip code, Olaf, right after the initials for the state."

"Well, Inga," Olaf complained, "they sure don't make it very easy for a feller to know that, do they? I worked so hard to find out how to write Florida and then they knock off five letters and add five numbers. I wonder if Ole Julson understands all this stuff down at the post office?"

Inga laughed and patted Olaf on the shoulder.

"I think he does, Olaf," she said. "Otherwise they wouldn't be keeping him in his job very long."

"I never thought of him as being all that smart when we were kids," Olaf said, "but maybe he had more brains than I gave him credit for."

Inga picked up the brochure again to examine it more closely.

"What is this you are filling out Olaf?"

"Oh this came in a letter that I got in the mail, Inga," Olaf said. "And it says that I am already a winner of a wonderful vacation at that fancy new resort in Miami, Florida."

Inga handed Olaf his brochure. "Is that the same place they have been talking about on the TV during the Packer Games, Olaf? They call it Heart's Ease."

"Ya, Inga!" Olaf replied. He waved the letter enthusiastically. "And this letter says that I am for sure a winner. It says that I have won a free vacation there for two people. I was thinking maybe Elden Sandstrom would go with me."

"Why that is nice of you to think of Elden," Inga offered. "He helped you get started on the garbage route, didn't he, Olaf?"

"Yah, Inga, he sure did." Olaf replied. "I thought Elden might have the money that we need to send with the application. He gets a pension check each month now that he is retired."

"It seems strange," Inga said, "that you have to send them money if you are the winner of a free vacation?"

"Inga," Olaf said, "they are not going to be sending valuable coupons all over the country for crooks to steal out of people's mailboxes. When we get to Miami they will check the numbers on our application and then we will get our money back. That's how Stella Olson explained it to me."

"So Stella and Alf are going?" Inga asked.

"Ya, they left a week ago Wednesday." Olaf explained. "they should be there now, enjoying all the pleasures of Heart's Ease."

"Let me see if I remember what those pleasures are," Inga said, beginning to sing and act out the advertisement she had seen each week on TV.

"Perfect weather,

not a cloud in your sky,
Sumptuous dining,
from main course to pie,
Endless service,
all day and all night,
When you come to Heart's Ease
your worries take flight."

"Why Inga," Olaf exclaimed, "I never knew you were watching those ads. Maybe you wanted to go to Heart's Ease. I'd rather go with you than with Elden Sandstrom."

"But you need Elden to pay the advance fees," Inga reminded him.

"Well, I really have the money myself, Inga," Olaf explained, a bit sheepishly. "I just thought if Elden would pay it I would let him. Then I wouldn't have to dip into my snuff money."

"Olaf!" Inga said, "I thought you had quit using snuff. You said you thought that Father would be pleased if you didn't use that anymore."

"Oh sure, Inga. I did quit using snuff," Olaf assured her. "But now I take the same amount of money that I used to pay for snuff, and put it in a jar. You'd be surprised how many jars I've got now."

Inga laughed as she reached out and clasped Olaf's hands.

"Oh Olaf, you are so funny sometimes. But I don't think I would go with you, Olaf. That place may call itself Heart's Ease but it won't ease the heart of anyone whose heart is really troubled."

"You wait, Inga!" Olaf said. "When Stella and Alf come back they will tell you what a wonderful place it is. Then you will wish you had gone …"

Olaf was interrupted by the ringing of the telephone. Inga stepped over and lifted the receiver.

"Hello!" Inga said. "Yes, this is Inga Ingabretson."

Inga winced and held the receiver farther from her ear.

"Who? Why sure I will, Alf. I hope nothing is the matter with Stella. Put her on … hello … hello, Stella. Are you okay? Oh good! Yes, he is here … yes, Stella, I'll get him right away. I hope you and Alf are having a good time in Heart's Ease … okay … yes … I will get Olaf right away, Stella …"

Inga covered the phone with her hand as she spoke to Olaf. "It is Stella Olson. She is quite excited. She wants to talk to you …"

Olaf took the phone and moved away from Inga for greater privacy. Inga resumed her examination of the Heart's Ease brochure.

Forgetting his desire for privacy, Olaf spoke loudly into the phone, trying to be heard in Florida.

"Hello Stella," he shouted, "can you hear me? Ya! … Ya! … You don't say … well what do you know about that? … Huh? … Ya! … Ya! …Why sure Stella … sure. Ya, I can do that … sure Stella. Okay Stella … Tell Alf hel …"

Olaf handed the phone to Inga sheepishly.

"Is something wrong, Olaf?" Inga asked as she put the phone back in its place.

Olaf reamed out his ear with his finger.

"I think you could hear as well as I could Inga, maybe better than I can hear now."

"It sounds like they weren't too happy with Heart's Ease, Olaf," Inga said.

"Ya well," Olaf began, "to start with they weren't the winners that they thought they would be."

"It is a good thing, then, that they had paid in advance." Inga offered, trying to make a bad situation better.

"They thought they had paid in advance," Olaf went on, "but that was only half of the fees, so Alf had to put the rest on their son-in-law's credit card that they took along for the trip."

"That must be so disappointing to them, Olaf," Inga said. "Did Stella say how the weather was?"

Inga was hoping to find a bright side to the situation. To no avail. Olaf needed to talk – as though that would relieve the ringing that Stella's voice had created in his head.

"Stella said it was too hot in the daytime and it rained all night," he reported. "She said that their room was small and stuffy and smelled like mold, and the sheets were only changed once all week. She said that Alf would have made a better cook than the ones they had at the resort."

"That is too bad, isn't it, Olaf?" Inga said sadly. "They had such high hopes for a good time in Heart's Ease."

"Ya!" Olaf replied. "Stella said if they ever get back here they will rename our town 'The Real Heart's Ease' and they'll never leave it again."

"I suppose they had to charge their flight home on their son-in-law's credit card," Inga suggested.

"No," Olaf said, "they had maxed out the credit card the first day, so they asked if I would telegraph them some money to come home on."

"And what did you tell them Olaf?"

"I said, 'Sure, Stella, I could do that.'"

"That is kind of you, Olaf, but now you won't have money for your trip to Heart's Ease."

Olaf shrugged. "Ya I know, Inga." Olaf thought a little while. "I think Stella is right. This is Heart's Ease right here where we live … if we let ourselves be at ease here."

"Oh Olaf," Inga said, "I'm so glad to hear you saying that. You are talking more like Father, every day."

"Thank you Inga," Olaf said. "That is what I want to do."

Compliments rarely came his way and they invariably embarrassed Olaf but he gladly took them when they came from Inga.

Olaf made a clumsy attempt to hug his sister. It was the first hug he had given anyone since childhood and he knew it was miserably ill-done. But when Inga started back to the kitchen, wiping a tear on her apron, she thought it was the dearest hug she had ever received.

"Inga!" Olaf called after her.

"Yes, Olaf! What is it?" she asked.

"Don't feel sorry for me," he said with a sheepish grin. "I will still have two jars of snuff money left."

Inga smiled at him. "I wish you would call it something else, Olaf . . . but I'm glad for you."

"Ya," Olaf responded, "and there will be a lot more soon. I used to buy a lot of that stuff."

Olaf crumpled the Heart's Ease brochure into a wad and tossed it to Inga. She caught it and headed to the kitchen to put it where it belonged.

The Family Albums

Olaf had spread the family albums on the table before him. As he turned the pages, he reentered a life that he had long ago run from. At times he paused to look at Inga and seemed about to speak to her. Inga had been busy with day-end chores, but he knew that she was about to settle down with her book for the evening.

When Olaf finally spoke to her, his tone was thoughtful.

"Inga," he said.

"Yes, Olaf," Inga replied, "what is it you want?"

"Inga," Olaf began again hesitantly, "I was looking at these pictures in your albums, and I was wondering why you never … well, why you have remained …"

Olaf turned full around in his chair and faced Inga.

"Well, I don't want to embarrass you, Inga, or make you feel bad …"

"Well, Olaf, I'm not too easy to embarrass," Inga said.

Inga knew it would take a push to get Olaf off the verbal cliff he was clinging to.

"If you say whatever you are wanting to say in a way that shows you love me, it won't make me feel bad. What is it that you want to know?"

"Well, Inga, I was wondering just now, as I looked at these albums, why you never married." Olaf hurried on to explain. "You were always so pretty, and everyone thought you were a wonderful person."

"Oh Olaf," Inga protested, "I can't say about that. I think there were plenty of people who didn't think I was so wonderful. There are plenty of people who still don't think I'm wonderful. But I could ask the same question about you, Olaf. Why didn't you ever marry?"

"That's not fair, Inga," Olaf protested, "I was asking you first, so it is my question that deserves the first answer."

"I'm sorry, Olaf. I didn't mean to be unfair."

Inga moved to the table and sat by Olaf. "It's just that your question took me by surprise and I needed some time to think about it."

Olaf directed Inga's attention to the album in front of him.

"I have been looking at the pictures in this album, Inga. See this one." He pointed. "Even when you were very young you were playing house, making things to please the rest of us. You would have made a wonderful wife for someone, Inga."

"Why, thank you, Olaf." Inga patted his hand, pleased with Olaf's compliment. "That's nice of you to say that."

"And look at this picture, Inga," Olaf continued. "You were beautiful when you went to the prom with Johnny Oldenberg. I always thought you would probably marry Johnny."

Inga picked up the album, looking at the picture wistfully. "Yes, Olaf," she said, still holding the album, "Johnny was a fine young man, and a perfect gentleman to be with … he still is a fine man."

"Then why didn't you marry him, Inga? I know that Johnny would have jumped at the chance to marry you."

"Well, I don't know about that, Olaf," Inga said. She placed the album on the table. "I loved Johnny too," she said, "but I wasn't put here on earth to be Johnny's wife."

"How can you say that, Inga?" Olaf protested. "You are just as much entitled to marry as anyone else …"

"Olaf, stop!" Inga said.

She placed her hand on his again and was silent for a while before speaking.

"When I was very young," she continued, "Father began to talk to me about the things that I would be and the things that I would do with my life. Sometimes I would be sad after those conversations. I wanted to be like every other person – to marry, have a family, maybe have a career – and enjoy a regular life."

"Then why didn't you do it, Inga?" Olaf insisted. "There was nothing to stop you? You could have married Johnny Oldenberg and still done all the things that you have done. Johnny would have been proud of you for all of them. And think of the wonderful children you would have had … and grandchildren too by now."

"Father said that what is good for one person may not be good for another," Inga explained. "In fact what is good for one person may be very bad for another."

She paused and looked away through the window before continuing.

"Father said that I was not to marry so that I could be a wife – sort of – a companion, to anybody who needed me; so I could be a mother – sort of – to many children."

"Ya, Inga," Olaf confessed, "Father used to talk to me like that too. He said that I *should* marry."

Olaf pulled one of the open albums close to them and turned a couple of pages.

"I just saw the picture of me and Hildi Olafson in the book here." Olaf said. He blushed and laughed self-consciously. "Everybody used to say that she would be Hildi Olafswife if she married me."

Inga laughed, patted Olaf's hand, and then got up to return to her work.

"Well, Olaf," she said as she resumed dusting the mantle. "I've always wondered why you didn't marry Hildi. She would have made a wonderful sister-in-law for me."

"Oh, Inga," Olaf said regretfully, "I wish that I could say that I had always done like you did … that I had done what Father told me I should do."

"Well, Olaf, why didn't you?"

"I think, Inga, I wanted to live my life for me." Olaf paused a while. "I wasn't very smart then, Inga. I am still not very smart, am I?"

"Oh, Olaf, it isn't a matter of how smart you are."

She laid aside her duster and returned to sit again by Olaf.

"What matters is how obedient you are to what Father wants you to do."

Olaf turned the pages of the album as he considered Inga's words.

"Ya, I think that is true, Inga," Olaf finally said. "Father told you that you should not marry so you could live your life for many others. He told me that I should marry so I could live my life for someone besides myself."

"That is a wonderful way to put it, Olaf," Inga said. "But it is never too late to be obedient to Father," she added.

"Well it sure is for me!" Olaf protested. "Hildi is already married and has ten grandchildren. And any of the other women I might have chosen are married too, or they have become …" Olaf hesitated. "Well, you know what I mean, Inga."

Inga patted Olaf's protruding stomach. "Well, Olaf," she said, "you have become … too."

They both laughed. "But there are other ways that you can be obedient to Father's will," Inga said.

"Really, Inga?" Olaf responded. "Tell me what you mean."

"Well, you said yourself that the reason you never married was because you wanted to live your life for yourself."

"Ya," Olaf admitted, "I'm not very proud of that now."

"Well then, you can start right away, living your life for others," Inga responded. "That is really what Father wanted you to do, whether you married or not."

"But Inga," Olaf protested, "does that mean that I can't go fishing when I want to, or can't watch the Packers anymore?"

"You have to decide that Olaf. You have to decide what is most important to you – your will, or Father's will."

"That is hard, Inga,"

"I know it is, but you can do it if you remember what you have learned from Father, and do what you think he would have you do."

"I know you are right," Olaf confessed. "I think I'm going to watch you more, Inga, and do things the way I see you do them."

"I only do the things I've seen Father do," Inga said. She stood up to resume her work.

"And, Olaf," she said, "I'll be here to talk to you anytime you need me."

"Thank you, Inga," Olaf said.

He turned a few pages in the album before him.

"You know, Inga," he said, "Sigrid Helmetson is still a pretty nice looking woman."

Inga smiled without pausing in her work.

"And a good woman too, Olaf," she said. "I hear that she has been looking for someone to help her out around her place since her husband died."

"Well," Olaf said, "a widow shouldn't have to hire someone when there are able bodied men around who could do the work for her."

"I agree." Inga said. "And I remember Father saying something like that too."

The Garbage Collector

When Olaf arrived home, tired and dirty from his garbage route, he found Inga in tears, sitting in the kitchen, holding a letter.

"Inga," Olaf said, going quickly to her side. "You are crying … what is the matter with you? Why are you crying?"

Inga had not seen Olaf enter, and even the sound of his voice did not immediately bring full awareness of his presence. She slowly looked up at him, then looked again at the letter in her hand. Her hand trembled as she lifted it in Olaf's direction.

"Olaf," she said, barely able to speak the words. "Have you seen this letter?"

"Why sure, Inga," Olaf replied. "I brought it in from the mail box yesterday. What do you think of it? Isn't that terrible stuff that mayor Swenson has been doing?"

"Oh Olaf," Inga countered. "I had hoped that you would be as sad about this letter as I am? Why aren't you sad about it?"

"Inga," Olaf said, "just read the letter! The letter tells you why it is important. The letter justifies itself."

"No Olaf," Inga replied. "This letter justifies nothing. It is a collection of gossip and lies and petty grievances. And then, on the basis of those things, it demands that mayor Swenson resign."

Olaf was stung by Inga's displeasure, but he was unwilling to give in.

"Yeah! Don't you think he should resign, Inga, if that many people are convinced that he is a crook; if he has done that many bad things to people?"

"Olaf, it isn't what is in the letter that makes me so sad," Inga said. "If these things are true that is too bad. If they are not true it is even more terrible that someone would say they are. But the thing that makes me sad is that someone would be so angry with mayor Swenson that they would write all of this and then not be willing to sign their name to the letter."

"Inga, you don't think someone would be willing to do that, do you?" Olaf asked. "You don't think someone would sign his own name to a letter like that? Think how it could hurt his reputation if things didn't go the way he wanted them to go. I know why he would not want to be known."

"I know too, Olaf," Inga said.

"What do you mean by that, Inga?" Olaf sensed that a trap was being set.

"I mean that I know why this person wants to be anonymous."

Olaf shrugged. "Whatever that means?"

Inga refused to be deterred by his put down.

"It means," she said, "that he lacks the courage to let himself be known, that he doesn't want to have to give answers to people for the things he has written. It means that he doesn't have the facts to back up his accusations."

"Well, Inga, what the letter says is true and you know that it is true!"

"I know that mayor Swenson is not perfect," Inga replied. "I know that he makes mistakes. But I know that he is a good man who will admit his mistakes when they are shown to him, and he will try to make amends with the people he has hurt."

There was a long silence before Inga spoke again.

"Olaf," she said. "I know who wrote the letter …"

"You do, Inga? How do you know that?"

"I can tell by the writing."

"Yeah, but that is not …" Olaf stopped mid-sentence, knowing that he was about to say more than he should.

"That is not *your* handwriting, Olaf? Is that what you were about to say?"

Olaf said nothing. Eventually Inga continued.

"I know it is not your handwriting, Olaf, but it is your *writing*. They are your words. You had one of your friends write it, I suppose, but you told him what to write."

Olaf had nothing to say. He knew that it was useless to lie to Inga. He waited uncomfortably for her to make the next move.

"Why did you do it?" she asked quietly.

Olaf made a few attempts to answer but each died in his mouth after a few fumbled words. He knew that truth was the only thing that would satisfy Inga.

"I found a letter when I was picking up Mrs. Vendmar's garbage." Olaf began. "It just fell out for me to see and I picked it up and read it while I was driving to the next place."

"Yes," Inga said, "and what was in the letter, Olaf?"

"Well, it was a letter from Mrs. Wright, who moved away two years ago," Olaf said. "And she was answering Mrs. Vendmar's letter about the things that Swenson had done to her and her husband. Mrs. Wright said that Swenson had done the same thing to her and her husband and that she knew a lot more things he had done to other people."

"Is that all, Olaf?" Inga prodded. "Just one letter?"

"No," he confessed, "I kept the letter and then, when I would see Mrs. Vendmar, when I was picking up her garbage, I just talked to her a bit each time. And little by little I learned a lot of things that mayor Swenson has been doing to people here in town."

"You have never liked mayor Swenson very well, Olaf, since he quit drinking with you and your friends several years ago." Inga paused. Olaf said nothing. "I remember how hard you and your friends worked against him the first time he was voted in as mayor."

"Inga," Olaf protested, "you know what a terrible person he was when we were younger. You know how he and his brothers were into all kinds of trouble when they were young. Have you forgot the terrible thing they did to you?"

"No, I have not forgotten that." Inga paused. "And I know that some of what you say is true."

Inga gazed at the letter a while before looking up at Olaf.

"He was your friend then, wasn't he?" she said. "You ran with him and his brothers and it grieved Father's heart that you did so." There was another prolonged silence. "But I know mayor Swenson is a different person now," Inga continued. "He has changed his ways and he is trying to do good things for the community that he one time was not very good to."

Olaf stood quietly, wishing he could find words to defend himself, or at least words that would make his actions less offensive to Inga.

"Olaf," Inga said, "what you are doing is not what Father would want you to do. Father would have you forgive mayor Swenson if he has hurt you. He would have you tell the truth about him … or better yet tell nothing at all about him. And he certainly wouldn't want you hiding behind an anonymous letter like this one." Inga held the letter out toward Olaf. "Father would tell you to go to mayor Swenson and talk to him man to man."

Olaf shuffled nervously but did not respond.

Inga held the letter out to Olaf again. Her face conveyed the meaning of her words. "Olaf, this is not worthy of one who bears our Father's name!"

"But Inga," Olaf protested, "it tells things that need to be …"

"Olaf!" Inga interrupted. "This makes me so sad and so ashamed."

Olaf remained silent for a long time while all the resistance drained away from him. Finally he was free to speak again.

"I am sorry, Inga," he said. "I didn't mean to make you sad. I didn't mean to dishonor

Father and you. I have made a mess of things, haven't I Inga?"

"But you can make it right, Olaf."

"How?"

Inga gripped Olaf's nearly lifeless arm.

"You need to let people know it was you who circulated this letter. You need to tell them how you got the information in it, and you need to apologize to those who were hurt by it. Especially you need to apologize to mayor Swenson," she added.

"But Inga, I will lose my job if I do that!" Olaf protested. "We are not suppose to be looking through the garbage as we pick it up. They will fire me if they know I did that!"

Inga would not relent. "Olaf," she said, "what would you rather have, your job as a garbage collector, or the respect and love of your friends in this community?"

Olaf took a deep breath and let it out slowly before answering.

"You are right, Inga," he said. "Thank you for showing me the right thing to do." He took Inga's hand. "It won't be easy, Inga. I don't know how to do it. Would you help me write a letter that says what I have done and how sorry I am for doing it?"

"Oh Olaf, that would be the thing I would most like to do with you today." she said. The tears that had clouded her eyes before seemed now to glisten.

"Shall we start right now?"

"Sure, Inga." Olaf wiped his eyes as he continued. "But I'll sign this letter … after we have said in it that you helped me write it," he added quickly.

Inga began to set up a place at the table for them to work on the letter. Olaf was still frozen to the place he had occupied since coming into the kitchen.

"Inga!" Olaf said.

Inga's heart stopped, afraid to hear that he was getting cold feet.

"Yes, Olaf, what is it?" she asked.

"You know, Inga," he said, "I just had the thought that they might not fire me from my job. I am the only one they have been able to keep on that route for longer than a year."

Inga laughed. "I think you may be right, Olaf. I hope they do keep you on the job. I know you enjoy driving that big truck."

"But if they don't fire me," Olaf said, "I know what I will tell the boss."

"What is that, Olaf?" Inga asked.

"I'll tell him I have learned my lesson. That from now on I'll take all the garbage straight to the dump where they can burn it, and bury its ashes, forever and forever!"

"Olaf," Inga laughed, "the longer you live here the more I see a resemblance of Father in you."

Mastering the Forward Button

"You are spending a lot of time with your new computer, Olaf." Inga was finishing up her evening chores but stopped to give her brother a friendly pat on the shoulder as she passed by. "I'm glad you've found something you enjoy to keep you busy in your retirement."

"Ya Inga, if I had worked as hard in school as you did I could probably write a book with this here thing. Max Leonard is writing his life story on his computer."

Olaf had turned to acknowledge Inga's attention. Inga gave him another pat on the shoulder.

"Well, the only thing that worries me, Olaf . . ." Inga hesitated, ". . . is that you seldom get out of the house now – to meet with your friends like you used to do."

"Oh we are talking all the time on the computer, Inga." Olaf turned back to the screen. "Max taught me how to use this e-mail program and we send e-mails back and forth all day long."

"I'm glad to know that you are writing to your friends, Olaf. Maybe you'll get good enough that you can write your book after all. What do you think you would write about?"

"Well, Inga, I'd probably tell the story of my life if I thought it would help anyone else to not live like I have lived."

"What do you mean, Olaf? Don't you think your life story would be interesting?"

"I think, Inga, that it might be a good story for some young punks who think they know everything there is to know. It might show them how that kind of thinking got me where I am today."

"And where would you say you are today, Olaf."

"Well, I'm right where I want to be now, Inga, living here with you in Father's house. But how I got here isn't a very pretty story. I'm not very proud of it. And what I had to bring with me when I moved back to Father's house was a lot of nothing."

"Oh Olaf, you didn't need to bring anything with you when you came back home. Father knew that nothing you'd have from your years of wandering would be worth keeping anyway. So everything you need is right here. And you are welcome to all of it."

"I know that Inga. And I'm glad for all the things I have here. But I regret some of the things I didn't do almost as much as I regret the things I did do."

"Like what, Olaf?"

"Well, for one thing I never learned to write good. I can't spell good, and I don't have good words to use, and when I try to write, the things I write don't make any sense at all."

"But I thought you said that you and your friends were writing to each other all day long on your computers."

"Well, I probably shouldn't have said we were writing. What we do is send e-mails back and forth that we get from other people. See, look at this Inga." Olaf displayed an e-mail he had gotten a few minutes earlier for Inga to look at.

"Let me get a chair, Olaf, so I can see better. That print on that screen isn't very large and my eyes aren't as good as they used to be." Inga pulled a chair alongside Olaf and began reading the e-mail.

"See, Inga. All I have to do is read the e-mail and then click on the word 'Forward' in the little square up at the top. Max Leonard fixed up my program so that when I click on 'Forward' it sends out the e-mail to thirty or forty people all at once. I don't have to write a single word and I've sent an e-mail to all those people."

Inga thought for a moment.

"That would be like if I took all the letters I received from my friends and put them in envelopes and mailed them off to other friends, huh Olaf? I don't think the people who send me letters would like that very much. Don't the people who wrote the letters get mad when they get sent all around like that?"

"No, Inga. You don't understand. Nobody writes these letters. Well, somebody must write them but nobody puts their name on the letters. They just write the letters and send them out so other people can send them on and eventually the whole country will have read their letter. Sometimes I wish I could write letters like they do."

"But I don't understand why grown men would spend their days sending letters from people they don't even know to other people who don't know them either."

"Inga, these are important letters. They tell people what is going on in this country and why they need to tell as many other people as they can. This is important stuff, Inga! We aren't just wasting our time with silly things. Here, just read this one."

Olaf clicked a couple of times and then turned the screen so Inga could read.

Inga read quietly while Olaf scrolled the screen down for her. Then she sat for a long time without speaking. A look of utter dismay had overtaken her face.

"What is wrong, Inga? You look disturbed. Don't you feel well?" Olaf reached over, laying a hand on Inga's arm.

"Olaf, this reminds me of another time, the time you and one of your friends wrote and circulated an anonymous letter defaming Mayor Swenson. Do you remember that time, Olaf? You said you had learned your lesson and you knew what to do with garbage from then on. I even helped you write a letter of apology to Mayor Swenson."

"Ya, Inga. I do remember that. That was not a good thing that I did, and I almost lost my job with the garbage company over it. It was only because you helped me write that letter that I got to keep my job."

Olaf paused, remembering his former offense, but then bristled with renewed animation.

"But these letters are different, Inga. I didn't write these letters. And nobody is making this stuff up. It is true what the letters say. You can tell by the way they are written."

"You are right, Olaf. 'Nobody' is making this stuff up. 'Nobody' would be ashamed to have his name known, so "Nobody" writes and sends these letters without any identification that would let someone write to him and ask him where he get his slanderous information."

"Inga, you wouldn't call this stuff slanderous if you had seen as many of these letters as I have. I have seen hundreds of letters and they all say the same thing. The President, and all the other people they are talking about in the letters are all crooks and if the citizens of our country don't wake up and throw them out we'll go down just like the Roman Empire did. We'll be taken over by Communists and all the good people will be herded into concentration camps and made to work until they are dead."

"Olaf," Inga laughed, "I don't think the Roman Empire fell to the Communists and I doubt if our country will either."

Inga paused and then continued in a sober mode.

"I don't know if the things in the e-mails you are reading and passing on are true or false. They sound false to me but one would have to look up the facts to know for sure. Do you ever look up the facts before you click on "Forward"?

"You know I don't read good, Inga. It is all I can do to read the e-mails and pass them on. If I had to look up the facts about each of them I wouldn't have any time to read the other e-mails."

"I suppose, when you are so sure the things you are reading are true, there isn't any reason to check whether they really are true, huh, Olaf?"

"That's right, Inga. It would be a waste of time." Olaf paused, then confessed. "Johnny Oldenberg sometimes sends me a letter saying that he has looked up the facts and that they aren't true. He always gives me a place to look and read for myself but I only did that a time or two. I didn't understand what they were writing about. They write pages and pages about it. They don't write as plain as the people who make the e-mails. And besides, Max Leonard says, 'How do you know those other people aren't liars?' So I just go on believing what I see with my own eyes, Inga."

"I think, Olaf, that you go on believing what you want to believe. Do you ever wonder how these e-mails affect the lives of the people they are denigrating?"

"I don't know what 'denigrating' is Inga. All I know is that they are people who are out to destroy our country and whatever happens to them can't be too bad."

"I'm asking if you ever think about how those people being criticized – and possibly lied about –feel when they know that letters like this are circulating around the country."

Olaf sat silently.

"Olaf," Inga continued, "we are both children of our Father. Father would never have condoned the writing of letters like these. He said he hated lies and slander and those who stir up trouble by the words they use. It makes my heart sad to see you passing on these kinds of accusations without even trying to know if they are true. And even if they are true, it makes me sad to know that they are being passed on from Father's house by one of Father's sons."

There was a long silence before Olaf spoke. His shoulders slumped and his eyes avoided Inga's.

"You know, Inga. I have been feeling a little guilty after reading some of the letters from Johnny Oldenberg. He does what you are saying I should do. He looks up the facts and most of the time he finds that the letters are full of lies."

"Then why do you send them on, Olaf? Do you think Johnny is a liar? Do you think the facts he finds are untrue?"

Another long silence ensued.

"I guess for a couple of reasons, Inga. For one thing I want to believe the letters are true. I never did like that man that got elected President. I dislike him so much I can't even say his name. And anytime I hear something bad about him I want it to be true."

"And what is the other reason?"

"Well, like I said, Inga, sometimes I believe that Johnny Oldenberg is right and the letters are a pack of lies. Sometimes I wish I didn't have to pass them on. But they always end saying something like, 'If you love God and your country, send this on to all your friends.' And besides . . ."

Olaf paused again, unwilling to admit what he had to say next.

"Yes, Olaf?" Inga urged.

"And besides, Inga, I don't know how to tell Max Leonard and the other guys to stop sending these e-mails to me. They are my friends, Inga."

"Your 'friends' have not always been a good influence on you, have they, Olaf."

Olaf didn't speak for a long time. When he did his voice trembled and there were tears in his eyes.

"You know that better than anyone else, Inga. You know what the Larson boys and the Swenson boys and I did to you. I'm so sorry for that, Inga."

"I wasn't thinking of what you and your friends did to *me*, Olaf. I was thinking of what your previous friendships *have done to you*. You said, yourself, that they left you with nothing when you finally came back to live in Father's house. And now these friends are taking away from you the most valuable thing that Father gave you when you came home to live in his house."

"What is that, Inga? What are they taking away from me?"

"Olaf, the most valuable thing we both have is our family name and all that goes along with living in Father's house. I am so glad to bear my Father's name. You said the same thing, Olaf, not long after you came to live here in Father's house. Everything we do and say reflects upon Father and our family name. When you came home your friends noticed a change in you over time, some even said you were beginning to look like your father, talk like your father, act like your father."

Olaf sat limply in his chair. His voice was subdued.

"I think I see what you are saying, Inga. This machine," Olaf pointed to the computer, "is making me less like Father; making me do things that Father would not want me to do."

"It isn't the machine that is doing that, Olaf. It is your love of your friends that is greater than your desire to be like Father. It is your hatred of your political enemies that is poisoning your attitudes and making you less and less like Father."

Olaf made several attempts to speak. At last he managed a choked whisper, almost a prayer.

"Oh Inga, I need your help again. Can you help me find the words to tell Max and the other guys that I don't want to get any more of their e-mails? And can you help me to think about those politicians the way that Father would think about them?"

Inga rose from her chair and, standing behind Olaf, placed her hands on his shoulders. As she leaned down to place a kiss on his head a tear anointed Olaf's upturned face.

"Of course I can, Olaf. I would love to do that. The first part will be easy. The second part may take some time. But when you learn to see all men and women as Father does, then you'll find your heart is less troubled and fearful of the things that are coming in the future."

"But Inga, what can I do with this computer. I spent a lot of my snuff money to buy that thing. I hate to just throw it out in the garbage. Would you like to have it, Inga?"

"No Olaf, I don't have any need for it. But I'll tell you what we could do with it."

"What is that, Inga?"

"First I could help you send an e-mail to everyone on that list of people that Max put on your machine, telling them that you don't want to be a part of spreading unfounded and anonymous rumors about other people anymore. You can tell them why if you want to. Or you can just tell them you want out of their gossip circle."

"And then we can give the computer away, huh Inga?"

"Or, Olaf, I could help you get started writing your life story on it."

"Oh Inga, that would be the very best thing I could ever do with it – and the best thing I could do with you too."

Olaf was silent for a while, before suddenly becoming animated again.

"Inga, don't get rid of that list of names that Max put on the computer."

"Why not, Olaf?"

"Well, when we get my life story written, I think I want to send it to all those people."

"That is a good idea, Olaf."

"Ya, Inga. And at the end of the story I'll write, 'If you love God and your country, send this to as many people as you can.'"

"Oh Olaf," Inga laughed, "Sometimes you make me so glad that you are my brother."

About The Author

James (Jim) Rapp is a retired public school teacher.

Previous to his 27 year teaching career he served as pastor of a congregation in River Falls, Wisconsin for six years. In the years since his retirement from teaching he served his church in Eau Claire, Wisconsin as Director of Drama for 12 years until May 2009.

Jim holds a Diploma in Theology from North Central Bible College (now North Central University) 1958, and a Master's Degree in History from University of Wisconsin-River Falls 1971, with his major area of interest being the Ancient Near East.

He has written seven dramas, five of which have been staged. In his twelve years as Director of Drama he co-directed, with Music Director, Cheryl Brandt, twenty-two adult musical dramas and nine children's musicals.

Jim is author of four books of poetry, *Perfect Imperfection, Sandals: The Journey of Abraham and Sarah and Hagar, Second Crop: More Poems by James D. Rapp*, and *Etcetera: An Eclectic Expression of Humors*. He is also author of *Sermon on the Mount: Brief Meditations*.

Jim lives with Alice, his wife of 56 plus years, in Eau Claire, Wisconsin.

www.ingramcontent.com/pod-product-compliance
Lightning Source LLC
LaVergne TN
LVHW050609100826
845148LV00015B/3198

* 9 7 8 0 9 8 2 8 5 0 7 7 0 *